Beauty and the Pea

Crabtree Publishing Company
www.crabtreebooks.com
1-800-387-7650

PMB 59051,
350 Fifth Ave., 59th Floor
New York, NY 10118

616 Welland Ave.
St. Catharines, ON
L2M 5V6

Published by Crabtree Publishing in 2013

Series editor: Louise John
Series Design: Emil Dacanay
Design: Lisa Peacock
Consultant: Shirley Bickler
Editor: Kathy Middleton
Proofreaders: Kelly McNiven, Crystal Sikkens
Notes to adults: Reagan Miller
Print and production coordinator: Katherine Berti

Text © Hilary Robinson 2013
Illustration © Simona Sanfilippo 2013

Printed in Canada/022013/BF20130114

First published in
2013 by Wayland
(A division of Hachette
Children's Books)

**Library and Archives Canada
Cataloguing in Publication**

Robinson, Hilary, 1962-
Beauty and the pea / written by Hilary Robinson ; illustrated by Simona Sanfilippo.

(Tadpoles: fairytale jumbles)
Issued also in electronic format.
ISBN 978-0-7787-1155-1 (bound).
--ISBN 978-0-7787-1159-9 (pbk.)

I. Sanfilippo, Simona II. Title. III. Series:
Tadpoles (St. Catharines, Ont.). Fairytale jumbles

PZ7.R6235Be 2013   j823'.914   C2012-908177-9

**Library of Congress
Cataloging-in-Publication Data**

Robinson, Hilary, 1962-
Beauty and the pea / written by Hilary Robinson ; illustrated by Simona Sanfilippo.
    pages cm. -- (Tadpoles: fairytale jumbles)
    Summary: At Pea Castle, the beast puts a pea under Beauty's mattress to see if she is the princess who can turn him back into a handsome prince.
    ISBN 978-0-7787-1155-1 (reinforced library binding : alk. paper) -- ISBN 978-0-7787-1159-9 (pbk. : alk. paper) -- ISBN 978-1-4271-9303-2 (electronic pdf) -- ISBN 978-1-4271-9227-1 (electronic html)
    [1. Stories in rhyme. 2. Characters in literature--Fiction. 3. Princes--Fiction. 4. Princesses--Fiction.] I. Sanfilippo, Simona, illustrator. II. Title.

PZ8.3.R575Be 2013
[E]--dc23
                                        2012047920

Beauty and the Pea

Written by Hilary Robinson
Illustrated by Simona Sanfilippo

Crabtree Publishing Company
www.crabtreebooks.com

A shopkeeper came to Pea Castle
and helped himself to a feast.
But little did he know that
Pea Castle was owned by a beast.

A wicked witch had cast a spell
on the beast, who was once a prince.

He had hidden away in Pea Castle
and has been lonely ever since.

The witch had said that a kiss and a pea
could be used for their magical powers
to turn the beast back into a prince
by a princess who liked flowers.

The shopkeeper slept at the castle
but, as he left, he plucked a red rose.

A booming voice said, "How dare you!"
The shopkeeper looked around and froze.

11

"You've slept and ate in my castle.
Now you've taken a rose from my door!
If you want to escape," said the beast,
"tell me who the rose is for!"

"For Beauty," the shopkeeper said, shaking.
"Your daughter?" asked the beast with a wink.

"Here! Take all the roses—the red and the white,
the yellow, and also the pink!"

"Give her all these, then bring her to stay here with me for a while."

The shopkeeper said he would do so,
and the beast turned away with a smile.

Perhaps, he thought, she's a princess,
and the shopkeeper is really a king.

As the beast walked around his gardens,
his aching heart started to sing!

He made up her bed with a mattress after putting a pea in its place.

He laid a rose on her pillow
and hung up curtains of lace.

Beauty stayed a week at Pea Castle,
to the beast's complete delight.

He asked if her mattress was comfy
and if she'd slept through the night.

"I'm sorry. I have not," said Beauty.
"There's such a big lump in my bed!"

Then the beast knew she was not just a girl, but a beautiful princess instead.

He jumped up with joy and said, "Beauty!
I know I look ugly and smell.
But please kiss me once on my head
to cast off a witch's mean spell."

27

Beauty did as he asked her,
and a prince appeared from the beast!

The very next day they were married...

... and served pea cake at the feast!

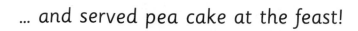

Tadpoles: Fairytale Jumbles are designed for transitional and early fluent readers. The books may also be used for a read-aloud or shared reading with younger children. **Tadpoles: Fairytale Jumbles** are humorous stories with a unique twist on traditional fairytales. Each story can be compared to the original fairytale, or appreciated on its own. Fairytales are a key type of literary text found in the Common Core State Standards.

THE FOLLOWING BEFORE, DURING, AND AFTER READING ACTIVITY SUGGESTIONS SUPPORT LITERACY SKILL DEVELOPMENT AND CAN ENRICH SHARED READING EXPERIENCES:

1. Make reading fun! Choose a time to read when you and the child are relaxed and have time to share the story.
2. Before reading, invite the child to preview the book. The child can read the title, look at the illustrations, skim through the text, and make predictions as to what will happen in the story. Predicting sets a clear purpose for reading and learning.
3. During reading, encourage the child to monitor his or her understanding by asking questions to draw conclusions, making connections, and using context clues to understand unfamiliar words.
4. After reading, ask the child to review his or her predictions. Were they correct? Discuss different parts of the story, including main characters, setting, main events, and the problem and solution. If the child is familiar with the original fairytale, invite he or she to identify the similarities and differences between the two versions of the story.
5. Encourage the child to use his or her imagination to create fairytale jumbles based on other familiar stories.
6. Give praise! Children learn best in a positive environment.

IF YOU ENJOYED THIS BOOK, WHY NOT TRY ANOTHER TADPOLES: FAIRYTALE JUMBLES STORY?